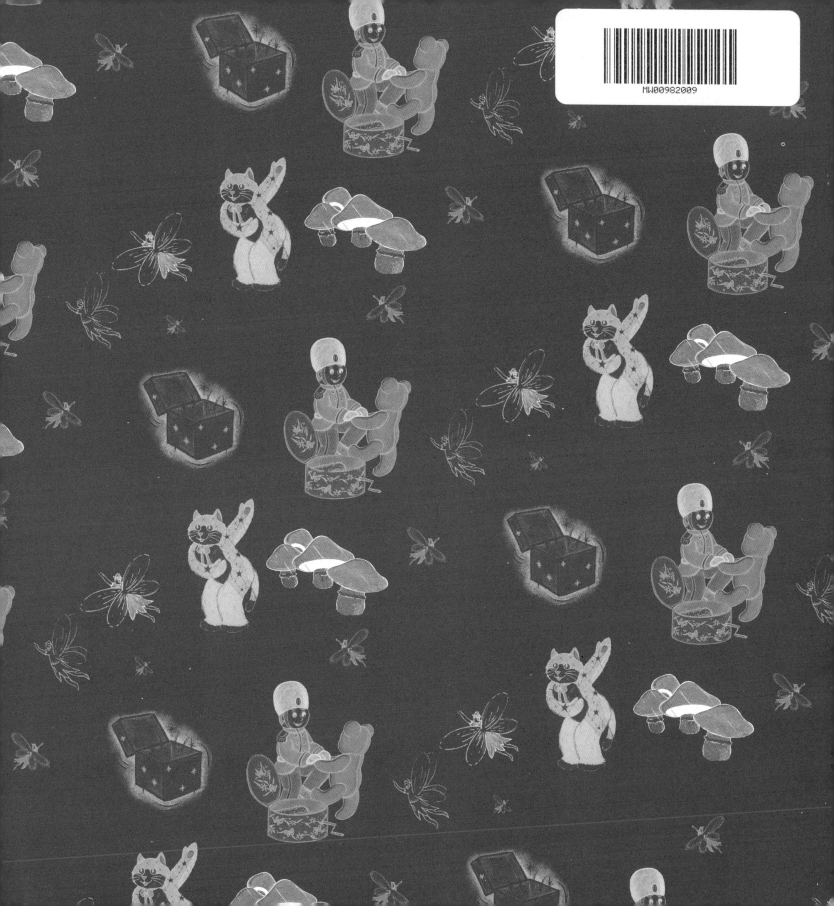

The
Adventurous
Ball
~ & ~
Poor Captain
Puss

Published in 2004 by Mercury Books London
20 Bloomsbury Street, London WC1B 3JH

© text copyright Enid Blyton Limited
© copyright original illustrations, Hodder and Stoughton Limited
© new illustrations 2004 Mercury Books London

Designed and produced for Mercury Books
by Open Door Limited, Langham, Rutland

Printed in China

Title: The Adventurous Ball & Poor Captain Puss
ISBN: 1 904668 33 X

# The
# Adventurous
# Ball
## ~ & ~
# Poor Captain
# Puss

MERCURY BOOKS
LONDON

# The Adventurous Ball

There was once a big round ball. It was all colours – red, yellow, blue, and green – and it looked very gay indeed when it bounced or rolled.

The other toys were rather impatient with the ball. They thought it a silly, dull creature. It could do nothing but bounce.

"What a life you lead!" said the sailing boat to the ball. "Nothing but bounce, bounce,

bounce! Look at me! I go sailing on the river and on the pond. I even go on the sea at seaside time!"

"And what about me?" said the toy bus. "When I'm wound up I go round and round the nursery, and I carry dolls, bears, and rabbits for passengers! I have a fine life!"

"And I fly up in the air and see all kinds of things!" said the toy aeroplane.

"So do I!" said the kite. "I fly above the clouds and see the birds up there, and get as near to the sun as I can get!"

"And we dolls get about a lot too," said the curly-haired doll. "We go out in prams – we are taken out to tea – we do see the world! Poor, dull ball, you do nothing but bounce. We are sorry for you."

The ball felt sorry for himself, too. He had never felt dull before the toys had said all this to him, but now he really did feel as if he led a miserable sort of life.

However, the time came when all that was changed, as you will hear. It happened that the children in whose nursery the toys lived went off to the seaside for a holiday, and with them they took most of their toys. The bus went, the dolls went, the aeroplane, the kite – and the ball. What fun!

And then the ball's adventures began. It had longed and longed for adventures, and it was surprised when it had some. It had been taken down to the beach and left on the sand whilst the children dug castles.

Nobody noticed that the tide had reached the ball. And no-one saw that it had taken away the ball when it began to go out again!

But it had! It bobbed the ball up and down on little waves, and took it right out to sea!

"Good gracious!" said the ball to itself. "I might be a little boat, the way I am floating along! Wherever am I going?"

A fish popped up its head and spoke to the ball. "Hello, big round fellow! What news of the land have you?"

The ball was proud to be able to tell news. It told the fish all about the other toys. Then the fish told the

ball about the sea, and all the fishes and other sea creatures in it. "You are a bold, brave ball to go adventuring off by yourself like this," said the fish. "I do admire you!"

The ball bobbed on, prouder than ever. Soon a big white sea-gull swooped down and came to rest just by the ball. "Hello, big round fellow,"  he said in surprise. "I thought you might be food. How very bold of you to come adventuring on the sea like this!"

The ball felt proud – but it was a truthful ball. "Well, as a matter of fact, I can't very well help this adventure," he said. "The sea took me away."

"Tell me news of the land," said the gull. So the ball told all about the other toys, and the gull then told him of the gulls, and of their seaweed nests, and young brown gull-babies. He told the ball of stormy days at sea. He showed him how he dived for fish. The ball was pleased and excited. How nice everyone was to him!

The ball bobbed in the pool and listened to the tales the crabs and shrimps told him. He heard about the children who came shrimping with a big net. He saw how the little crabs could bury themselves in the sand in two twinks and not show even a leg. It was all very wonderful to the big ball.

When the tide went out again the ball went with it. It bobbed along merrily. Suddenly it saw a great big thing coming straight at it. Oh dear, oh dear – it was an enormous steamer! The ball felt sure it would be squashed to bits – but at the last moment it bobbed to one side and the big steamer sailed on. "Look! Look!" cried the people on the steamer, leaning over the side.

"There is a fine big ball, bobbing along all by itself!"

The ball was proud to be noticed by the people on the steamer. It bobbed after it for a long way but then got left behind. The tide took it once more and some great big waves curled over it and almost buried it. But it bobbed up gaily again; wondering what adventure it would have next.

As it floated along it saw a little boat with two children in. "Look! Look! There's a beautiful big ball!" cried the boy. "Let's get it!"

The ball floated on. The tide turned again and flowed into a big bay. The ball floated by a boat and stayed there for a while. The boat spoke to him and told him how he sometimes went out fishing and how little boys and girls went rowing in him and used him for bathing.

The ball had never known such a lot of things in his life. He would have stayed by the boat for a longer time, but a little wave came and took him away. He floated into a rock pool, and there the crabs and shrimps swam up to him in admiration.

"What a fine big round fellow you are!" they said. "Where do you come from? How brave of you to adventure all alone on the big, big sea!"

The boat was rowed after the ball. The boy leaned out and took it. He shook the water from it and showed it to his sister.

"Do you know, Winnie, I believe it is our very own ball – the one we lost yesterday!" said the boy. "See the colours on it! I am quite sure it is our own ball!"

"So it is!" said the girl. "I wonder where it has been all this time! I wish it could tell us its adventures. I expect it has had such a lot, bobbing up and down on the sea."

The children
took the ball back
to shore. There were all
the other toys – the aeroplane, the bus, the
dolls, the kite, and all the rest. How surprised
they were to see the ball again!

"We saw you floating away!" cried the aeroplane. "Where did you go?"

"Ah," said the ball proudly. "I'm a big round adventurous fellow, I am! I've talked with birds and fishes, crabs and shrimps – I've heard tales from boats – I've nearly been run down by a great steamer, and all the people on it saw me! You may think I'm a dull fellow and can do nothing but bounce – but you are mistaken – I can float too – and I've had more adventures than the whole lot of you put together!"

And after that, as you can imagine, none of the toys ever laughed at the ball again for being a dull fellow who could do nothing but bounce! He could tell more stories than anyone else – and he says he is going to float away again next year and have some more adventures. I wonder if he will!

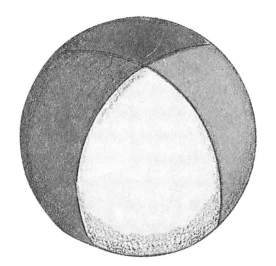

# Poor Captain Puss!

**R**onald and Jill were very lucky. In the summer they always went to Cliffsea, where their father had a house almost on the beach. It was such fun to wake up in the morning and hear the waves splashing on the sands not far off.

All the household went to Cliffsea in the summer, even Toby the dog and Patter the kitten! No-one was left behind. Toby liked the sea very much, and Patter loved playing about in the sand.

Next door to the children's house was a smaller one, and two cats and a dog lived there with their mistress. The dog was called Spot, and the cats were called Sooty and Snowball. So you can guess what they were like to look at.

Toby, Patter, Sooty, Snowball, and Spot were soon good friends. Patter the kitten had a fine time with them. They made quite a fuss of her because she was the smallest and youngest.

So she was rather spoilt, and she became vain and boastful. Ronald and Jill spoilt her, too, and said she was just the cleverest kitten they had ever seen.

"See how she runs after my ball!" said Ronald, as Patter raced over the sand to get his ball.

"See how Patter plays with this bit of seaweed!" said Jill. "She fetched it off the rocks for me, Ronald. She is a clever kitten! She can do simply anything."

Patter felt very clever indeed. She went about with her head in the air and began to think that the other animals were rather stupid.

But there was one thing she would not do! She wouldn't go paddling and bathing with the children as Toby and Spot did. No – she hated the water.

She thought it was simply horrid to get her dainty little feet wet.

Then one day Ronald and Jill bought down a beautiful big ship to the beach. It was a toy one, but was so big that Toby and Spot could almost get into it. Ronald and Jill played happily with it all morning, and sailed it on the rock-pools that were spread all over the beach.

When they went indoors to dinner the five animals crowded round the pretty boat.

"I wish I could sail in it!" said Toby. "I'd love to sail over that pool. I would make a good captain!"

"So would I," said Spot, wagging his tail and sniffing at the boat as it stood half upright in the sand.

"I would make the best captain!" said Patter the kitten boastfully. "Ronald and Jill are always saying what a clever kitten I am. I am sure I could sail this ship much better than any of you!"

"Why, Patter, you little story-teller!" cried Snowball. "You know how you hate to get your feet wet! You wouldn't be any good at all at sailing a boat."

"Yes, I should," said Patter crossly. "I know just what to do. You pull that thing there – the tiller, it's called – and the boat goes this way and that. I heard Ronald say so!"

"You don't know anything about it at all," said Sooty scornfully. "You are just showing off as usual!"

"I'm not!" mewed Patter angrily. She jumped into the boat and put her paw on the tiller. "There you are," she said. "This is what makes the boat go!"

The others laughed at her. They were sure that Patter would hate to go sailing really. They ran off and left her. She stared after them crossly, and then she lay down in the boat in the warm sunshine. She wouldn't go and play with the others if they were going to be so horrid to her. No, they could just play by themselves!

Patter shut her eyes, for the sun was very bright. She put her nose on her paws and slept. She didn't hear the sea coming closer and closer. She didn't know the tide was coming in! It crept up to the boat. It shook it a little. But Patter slept on, dreaming of sardines and cream.

Toby, Spot, Sooty and Snowball wondered where Patter was. They couldn't see her curled up in the ship. They thought she had gone indoors in a huff.

"She is getting to be a very foolish little kitten," said Toby. "We must not take so much notice of her."

"It is silly of her to pretend that she would make such a good sailor," said Sooty.

"Everyone knows that cats hate the water."

"Well, we won't bother about her any more," said Snowball. "She's just a little silly. Let's lie down behind this shady rock and have a snooze. I'm sleepy."

So they all lay down and slept. They were far away from the tide and were quite safe.

But Patter was anything but safe! The sea was all round the ship now! In another minute it would be floating! A great big wave came splashing up the beach – and the ship floated! There it was, quite upright, floating beautifully!

The rock-pool disappeared. It was now part of the big sea. The ship sailed merrily on it. It bobbed up and down on the waves.

Patter suddenly woke up, and wondered why things bobbed about so. She sat up and saw that she had fallen asleep in the boat – and when she looked over the side, what a shock for her! She was sailing on the sea! Big waves came and went under the boat. The beach was far away!

"Miaow!" wailed Patter. "Miaow! I'm out at sea! I'm afraid! I shall drown!"

But no-one heard her. The sea was making such a noise as the tide came in. Patter forgot how she had boasted about being a good sailor. She forgot that she had boasted she could sail the boat quite well. She just clung on to the side and watched with frightened eyes as the green waves came and went.

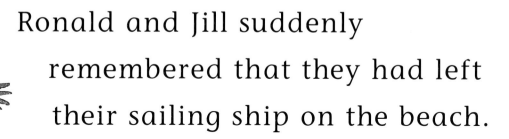

Ronald and Jill suddenly
remembered that they had left
their sailing ship on the beach.

"My goodness! And the tide's coming
in!" said Ronald in dismay. "Quick,
Jill, we must go and see if our boat is
safe!"

They ran from the house to the beach
– and then saw the tide was right in. And,
far away, on the big waves, floated their
beautiful ship, all by itself!

"Look!" cried Jill. "There it is! But there is someone in it. Who is it, Ronald?"

Ronald stared hard. Then he shouted out in surprise: "Why, it's Patter the kitten! Yes, it really is! Look at her in the boat Jill!"

"Oh, the clever thing!" cried Jill, who really thought the kitten was sailing the ship. "Oh, whoever heard of a kitten sailing a boat before? Spot, Toby, come and look at Patter sailing our ship!"

Spot, Toby, Sooty and Snowball awoke in a hurry and ran to see what all the excitement was about. When they saw

Patter the kitten out in the boat, rocking up and down on the sea, they could hardly believe their eyes. "Captain Puss is sailing the boat," said Jill. "Captain Patter Puss! Isn't she clever?"

But Spot didn't think that Patter was as clever as all that. His sharp ears had caught a tiny mew – and that mew was very, very frightened. It wasn't the voice of a bold captain – it was the mew of a terrified kitten!

"I believe she went to sleep in the boat and the tide came and took it away," wuffed Spot to Toby.

"Well, it will do her good to see that she isn't such a marvellous captain after all!" Toby barked back.

"She would be silly enough to fall asleep just when the tide was coming in," said Sooty.

"All the same, she's very frightened," said Snowball, who had heard two or three frightened mews.

"Sail the boat to shore, Patter!" shouted Ronald.

"Sail her in! We don't want to lose her!"

But Patter was much too frightened to pay any attention to what was said. She just went on clinging to the side of the boat. She felt very ill, and wished that she was on dry land.

Spot was quite worried. He knew what a little silly Patter really was – but all the same he thought she had been frightened quite enough. What could be done?

"I'll go and fetch her," wuffed Spot, and he plunged into the sea. He swam strongly through the waves, which were now getting quite big, for the wind had blown up in the

afternoon. Up
and down
went Spot,
swimming
as fast as he
could, for he

was really rather afraid that the ship might

be blown over in the wind – and then what

would happen to Patter!

The boat was a good way out. The wind blew

the white sails strongly. The waves bobbed it

up and down like a cork. Patter was terribly

frightened, for once or twice she thought the boat was going over.

And just as Spot got there, the wind gave the sails such a blow that the boat did go over! Smack! The sails hit the sea, and the boat lay on its side. Splash! Poor Patter was thrown into the

water. She couldn't swim – but Spot was there just in time! He caught hold of her by the skin of her neck and, holding her head above the water, he swam back to the shore. The ship lay far out to sea on its side.

Spot put poor, wet, cold Patter on the sand, and shook himself. Patter mewed weakly.

The others came running up to her,

"Well, you didn't make such a good sailor after all," said Sooty.

"Don't say unkind things now," said Snowball. "Patter has been punished enough. Come into the house, Patter, and sit by the kitchen fire and dry yourself."

Ronald and Jill watched the five animals running into the house. Then Ronald turned up his shorts and went wading into the water to see if he could get back his boat.

"That kitten was silly!" he said. "She took my boat out to sea, couldn't sail it back again, made it flop on to its side, and fell out herself! She isn't so clever as she thinks."

He got back his boat and went to dry the sails in the kitchen. Patter was there, sitting as close to the fire as she could, getting dry.

"Hullo, Captain Puss!" said Ronald. "I don't think you are much of a sailor!"

"No, she is just a dear, silly little kitten," said Jill.

Patter felt ashamed. How she wished she hadn't boasted about being a good sailor! She wondered if the others would ever speak to her again.

They did, of course, and as soon as they found that she wasn't boastful any more they were as good friends as ever.

But if Patter forgets, they laugh and say, "Now, Captain Patter! Would you like to go sailing again?"